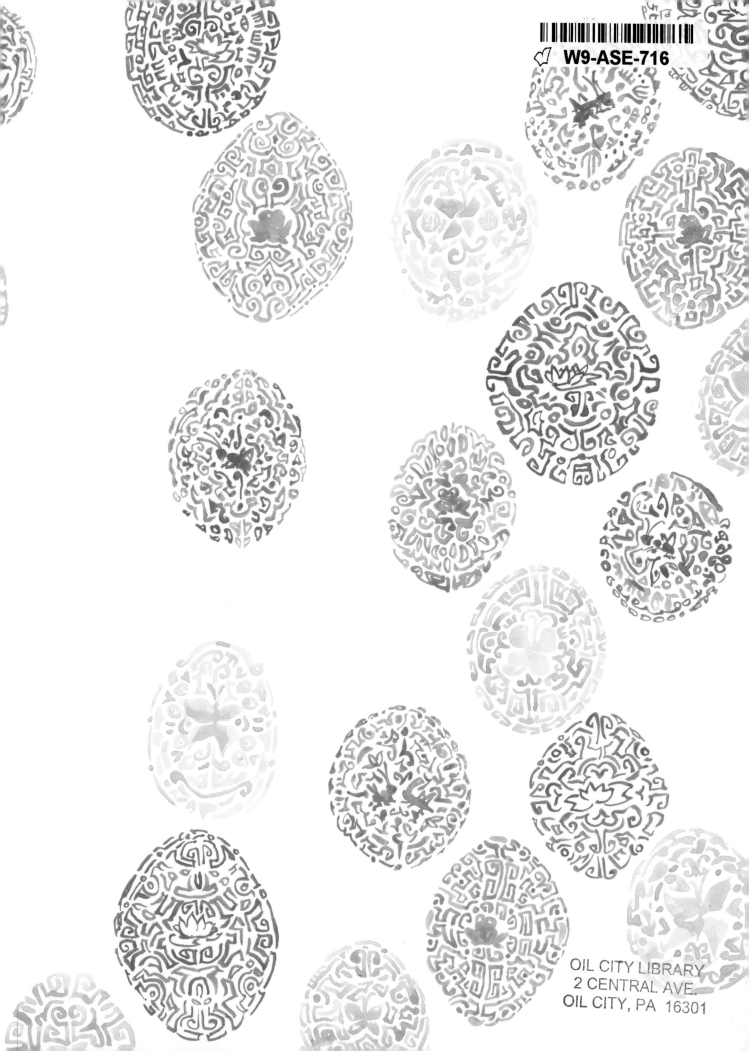

PEACE, BUGS,
AND UNDERSTANDING

For Chelsea. With thanks to metta makers, Sylvia Boorstein
and Sharon Salzburg, and to the Garrison Institute of New York. -GS

For our family known and unknown, in Vietnam and around the world.
-Youme

PEACE, BUGS, AND UNDERSTANDING:

An Adventure in Sibling Harmony

GAIL SILVER;

ILLUSTRATED BY
YOUME NGUYEN LY

E

PLUM BLOSSOM BOOKS
PARALLAX PRESS
BERKELEY, CALIFORNIA

Lily was having a picnic with her father and her little sister, Ruby, but it wasn't much fun. Ruby was lying on the checkerboard.

"Get off, Ruby," Lily said and pushed her sister.

"Hey, take it easy," said her father. He scooped Ruby into his arms.

Lily kept her head down and cleaned up the pieces, some of which were pennies and nickels because Ruby had lost the checkers. Then she folded the board back into its box, which was more flat than box shaped because Ruby had been sitting on it.

It's not fair, Lily thought. "Ruby ruins everything and she gets all the attention."

Lily looked around for something fun to do, but there wasn't anything. She folded her arms and looked over her shoulder at her sister. Sometimes Lily wished Ruby would just disappear.

"Did you see this?" said her father. He slid a book from the stack in the picnic basket and handed it to Lily.

"It looks like a journal," Lily said, flipping through its pages, "but with drawings."

"It is a journal," said her father. "It was my grandfather's."

Lily stopped at a sketch of a boy on a bicycle. In the background was a lily pond, and at the top of the page in faded pencil, was the date:

June 4, 1923.

"Wow, that was a long time ago," Lily thought. She settled down on the picnic blanket and began to read.

June 4, 1923

Today started out like any other day. It was warm and damp from the morning rain, and I was in in my secret hideout counting crickets.

That's when my sister barged in.

"Get out, Cam," I said. "You can't be here."

"Yes I can," she insisted.

"No you can't!" I shouted, "GO AWAY!"

"Mama!" Cam called, running toward the house.

I already knew how this would turn out.

"Lanh?" my mother called. "Let your sister play with you."

"But, Mama . . . it's my—!"

"Let her in, Lanh!"

"It's not fair!" I shouted. "She always gets—"

"I said, let her in. Now!"

Cam ran back in, kicking dirt and soot all over my fort. The crickets jumped out and I did too. I ran to the end of the yard, to my bicycle, and rode away from home.

The road through the village was muddy, and each time I saw a puddle, I made sure to ride through it. Standing up on the pedals, I soared past the town, past the people.

WHOOSH went the world.

The further I rode, the taller the grass grew.
Soon it was taller than I was, and it was filled
with the chirping of crickets and frogs. The
mud was thick, and I was tired and hot, but I
pushed and pedaled until I made it to the end
of the path, to a pond covered with . . .

"Water lilies," Lily whispered.

At the pond's edge, I used a stick to poke at a water lily and its tangled roots. I was hoping to find a frog or turtle or something, but all that was there was my own face, flushed and mud-splattered, staring back at me from the water.

"Nothing's going right today," I grumbled, and threw the stick at my reflection.

"Ouch!" someone said.

I jumped back, and looked around the pond. "Who said that?" I called out. "Who's there?"

"It's me of course," said the voice, "over here."

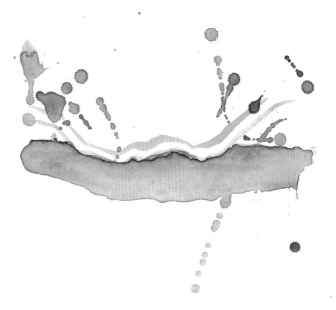

Perched on top of the lily pad was a strange looking frog-like creature.

"Who are you?" I asked. "And where did you come from?"

"You should know. You woke me."

"I didn't mean to wake anybody," I said.

"That's what they all say: I didn't mean to, Anger . . . I couldn't help it, Anger . . . It wasn't my fault, Anger, blah . . . blah . . . blah . . . blah . . . blah!"

"Wait a minute! You're my anger?"

"Who else would I be?" Anger said, and brushed some pondweed from his slick skin.

I looked carefully at the creature, at his bulging eyes, his dark green skin, and his webbed fingers and toes.

"Here," he said to me, and extended the stick across the water. "Can you give me a hand?"

"I was sort of hoping to be alone," I told him.

"But we are alone," said Anger.

"No, I meant ALONE alone. Can't you just go back to wherever you came from?"

"I wish I could, but it's not up to me," said Anger. "Now, grab hold, would you?"

I took the other end of the stick, and as I pulled it toward me, Anger leapt through the air, across the water, and landed right in my arms.

"I think you're going to have to take care of me for a little while," Anger said.

"I don't want to take care of anyone," I told him.

I tried to shake him off, but it was no use. He wouldn't let go.

The more I ignored him, the more of a nuisance he became.

"Anger," I finally said, "you're getting heavy and I don't feel so good. There must be something that I can do to get you off my back."

Anger loosened his grip around my shoulders and slid to his feet.

"Now that you mention it, there is something you can do."

"Why didn't you tell me before?"

"You weren't ready before."

"Well, I'm ready now."

"Okay," said Anger, "but you might not like it."

"I'll like it! I promise! Just tell me! What is it? What do I have to do?"

Anger plopped to the ground and crossed his legs.

"If you want me to go away," he said, "you have to find Metta."

"Who's Metta?" I asked.

"Metta's not a 'who,'" Anger said, scratching his ear.

I shielded the sun from my eyes, and scanned the pond, the way a sea captain would scan the sea, but I didn't know what I was looking for, and a bug almost flew into my eye.

Another one zigzagged in front of us. "There seem to be all kinds of pests out today," Anger said.

"Tell me about it! They won't leave me alone." A bug flew over my head and I flapped my arms, trying to shoo it away. "Go away, get out of here!" I yelled.

"I can help," Anger said, and he snatched up the bug with a quick swoop of his hand.

"You shouldn't do that," I told him.

"Why not?" Anger asked, "I thought it was bugging you!"

"Yeah, but you might hurt it."

"So," Anger shrugged. "It's just a bug!"

"All that for a stupid bug," Anger said, shaking his head.

I closed my eyes and tried to rest, but Anger was chomping on a piece of lemongrass and hiccuping loudly in between bites.

"Can you be quiet?" I asked him.

"I don't know," he said. "Can you?"

I sighed, and leaned back. My clothes were wet and my
sandals were squishy, but the sun was warm against my
skin, and I liked that.

"It's sort of nice here," I whispered. "Look at all the
butterflies."

"I don't care much for butterflies," said Anger.

"I like them," I said, and in the quiet of the afternoon, I watched them fly around the pond. The air smelled like pineapple, and all I could hear was the sound of my breath moving in, and slowly back out. "Cam likes them too," I said.

Anger yawned. He stretched his long legs out in front of him and, resting his head on a rock, he closed his eyes.

I kicked off my shoes and let my feet disappear in the grass. I didn't know what else to do, so I just kept breathing in and breathing out, thinking about butterflies and bugs, *breathing in and breathing out* . . . and things that were smaller than me, *breathing in and breathing out* . . . and how I didn't want Anger to hurt them.

I waited for Anger to say something, but he just breathed alongside me, *in and out*, his hands folded on his belly, a yellow butterfly on his toe.

"Cam would like that butterfly," I said softly. "Yellow's her favorite color."

Breathing in, breathing out, "May Cam be happy,"
I thought.
   Breathing in, breathing out, "May Cam be safe."
   Breathing in, breathing out, "May Cam be strong."
   Breathing in, breathing out, "May Cam live with peace."

I wonder what she's been doing while I've been gone.

   Breathing in, breathing out . . .

She better not be in my clubhouse.

   Breathing in, breathing out . . .

It's probably getting late. I have a long way home.

Lily closed the journal and sat up. "Ruby," she said excitedly, "can I read this to you?" But Ruby didn't answer. She wasn't there. On the corner of the blanket where Ruby had been, sat a big brown toad.

Lily gasped.

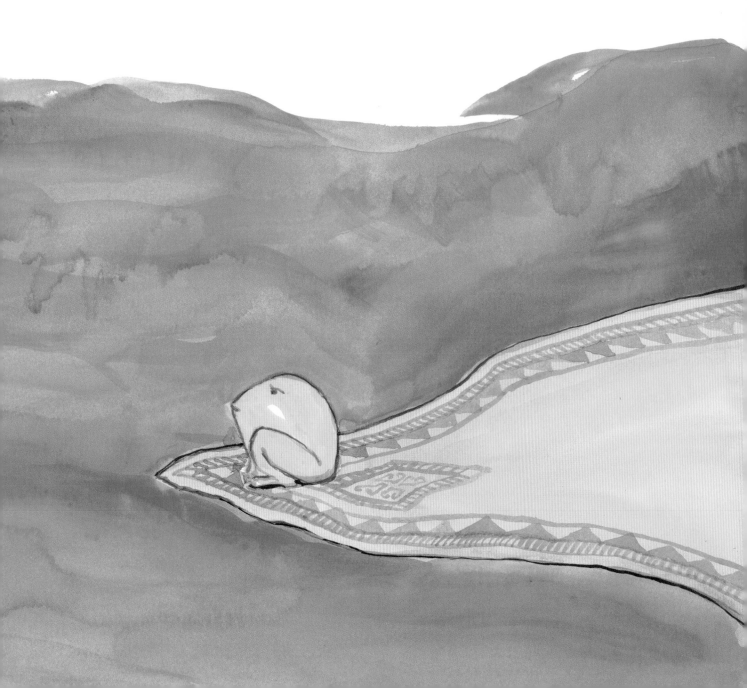

"Don't worry," her father laughed. "Ruby's right there."
He pointed to a shady spot under the tree, where Ruby
was curled up and asleep, her head resting on the flattened
checker box.

Lily knelt beside her sister. "May you be happy," she
whispered, and she kissed her sister on the cheek.

"May you be safe," she said.

"May you be strong," she said, and she tucked Ruby's
little bear under her arm.

"And may you live with peace."

Under the shade of the tree, Ruby smiled.
"It's good having a sister," she thought, and
she gently brushed away two butterflies that
had landed on her hand. They flew off, chasing
each other over the water lilies and across
the pond.

METTA

The word "Metta" comes from a very old language called Pali. It translates into English as "loving kindness" and, in practice, it is a strong wish for the happiness of others. When you practice Metta, sit quietly and become aware of your breath. Listen to how your breath sounds, or how it feels, moving in and out of your body. Then think about the person you want to wish kindness and recite your Metta wish for them as many times as feels good.

May you be happy.
May you be strong.
May you be safe.
May you live with peace.

You can practice Metta for lots of different people, for yourself, and even for the whole world at once. Practicing Metta is not just a way of being kind to other people, but it also helps to quiet our own anger and to cultivate forgiveness

toward others. I hope that practicing Metta brings peace to you and your family.

1.   Why do you think Anger said to Lahn, "I think you're going to have to take care of me for a little while?"

2.   What is Metta?

3.   What kinds of things bug you? What do you do when these things happen? What do you wish you had done when these things happened?

4.   Do you think you have to be angry to practice Metta?

5.   Do you ever do things that bug someone else? How do they respond?

6.   Why do you think Anger closed his eyes when Lanh started thinking kind thoughts? Why didn't he just disappear?

RELATED TITLES

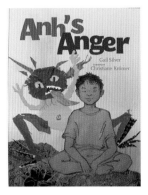

Anh's Anger
Gail Silver

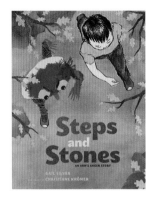

Steps and Stones
Gail Silver

Is Nothing Something?
Thich Nhat Hanh

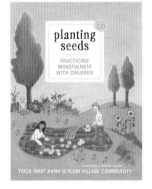

Planting Seeds
Thich Nhat Hanh

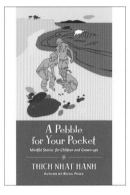

A Pebble for Your Pocket
Thich Nhat Hanh

A Handful of Quiet
Thich Nhat Hanh

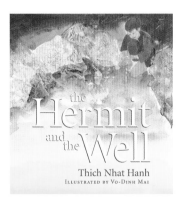

The Hermit and the Well
Thich Nhat Hanh

Plum Blossom Books, the children's imprint of
Parallax Press, publishes books on mindfulness
for young people, parents, and educators.

PARALLAX PRESS
P.O. BOX 7355
BERKELEY, CALIFORNIA 94707

PARALLAX.ORG

Plum Blossom Books is the
children's imprint of Parallax Press.
Text © 2014 Gail Silver
Illustrations © 2014 Youme Nguyen Ly
All rights reserved
Printed in Malaysia

Edited by Rachel Neumann
Illustrated by Youme Nguyen Ly
Cover and interior design by Debbie Berne

Library of Congress Cataloging-in-Publication Data

Silver, Gail.
Peace, bugs, and understanding : an adventure in sibling
harmony / Gail Silver ; illustrated by Youme Nguyen Ly.
pages cm
ISBN 978-1-937006-63-1 (hardback)
I. Youme, illustrator. II. Title.
PZ7.S58567Pe 2014
[E]--dc23
2014009438

1 2 3 4 5 / 18 17 16 15 14

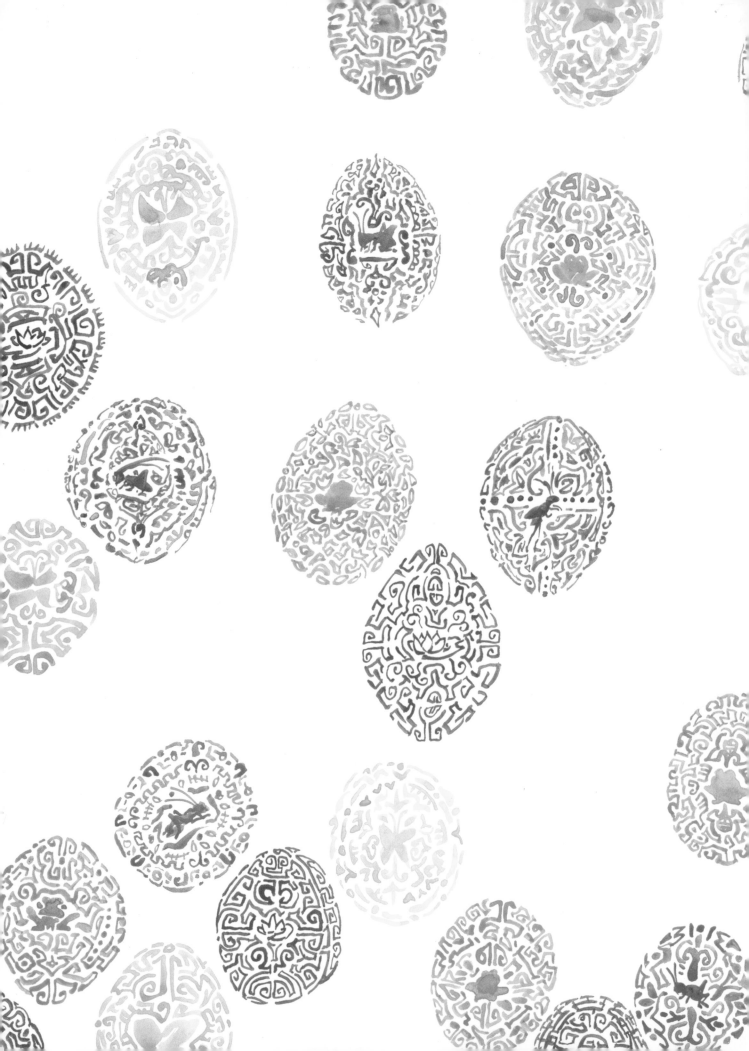